I0771670

A FIELD GUIDE TO THE SOUTHERN FAERIE FOLK

A Fun and Informative Manual Documenting the Mystical Creatures Living in the Southern United States

Written and Illustrated by Andy Triemer

This book is dedicated to my lovely and supportive wife Helen.

Special thanks to all of my Kickstarter backers and to Jason Triemer and Edea Triemer whose skills and talents were a great help in making this book a reality.

Published by Diddleho Studio

A FIELD GUIDE
to the
SOUTHERN FAERIE FOLK

TABLE OF CONTENTS

FOREWARD

Howdy! My name is Ned the Gnome and I'm what you'd call a mountain gnome. You may be wondering, what or who are the southern faerie folk? Well I'm here to explain this to you.

Have you ever heard of the realm of the faerie? It's most often associated with the countries in Europe: England, France, Norway, Sweden, etc. While it is a natural domain, it's also a magical place where fantastic and mystical creatures abide. A place that elves, fairies, gnomes and many other creatures call home. Many believe that this province is just a fantasy and not a real place, but I'm here to tell you that it is real! It is a dimension that is right here in the United States. You may have experienced the realm yourself during a quiet forest walk or as you watched the sun set over a shimmering lake. And it is entirely possible that you may have encountered some of the creatures, like a gnome such as myself that come from the world of the faerie.

This guide will describe some of these fantastic creatures. Specifically, the ones that can be found in the Southern United States. And while some of these creatures may be familiar to you, some may not. To help you as you perform your own field work, we have included a handy "Observation Notes" page at the start of each section. So enjoy this guide as you learn about the fascinating world of the fantastic southern faerie folk!

-Ned

WHERE ARE THE SOUTHERN FAERIE FOLK LOCATED?

As this guide is focused on the enchanted creatures in the southern region of the United States; it includes fae from fourteen southern states. These states are included on the map above with a brief description of their territory on the following page.

The South, as it is commonly referred to, is a diverse land of flatlands, marshes, swamps, lakes, and rivers as well as foothills and mountains. Additionally, with its relatively warm weather, the growing season is long and the plant life is luscious. This diverse landscape is the ideal habitat for many fantastic beings.

Alabama - Landscape includes, swamps, rolling hills and pine belts ranging from the foothills of the Appalachian Mountains in the north to the Gulf Coastal Plain in the south.

Arkansas - Includes features with rivers, mountains, forests, lakes, and bayous from the Ozark and Ouachita Mountains, to the Gulf Coastal Plain.

Florida - With swamplands, pine forests, fresh water rivers and lakes, the state is relatively flat with its highest point being 345 feet above sea level.

Georgia - With the Blue Ridge Mountains in the North, the Piedmont Region mid-state and the Okefenokee Swamp in the south, the variety of features includes mountains, foothills, rivers, lakes and swampland.

Kentucky - The state consists of fertile lands in the Bluegrass region, as well as extensive forests, rolling hills, and caves.

Louisiana - Its coastal plain along the Gulf of Mexico includes marshes and swamps, while the Mississippi River's alluvial plain contributes to its unique topography.

Mississippi - Featuring the lowland plains and low hills of the Gulf Coastal Plain, along with the fertile region of the Mississippi River Delta.

North Carolina - The state encompasses the Appalachian Mountains, the central Piedmont Plateau and the eastern Atlantic Coastal Plain with marshlands and beaches along the Atlantic Ocean.

Oklahoma - The state includes the Ozark Mountains, Wichita Mountains, Ouachita Mountains, and the Flint Hills and more than 500 named creeks and rivers, along with 200 lakes.

South Carolina - The state includes diverse geography with the marshes and coasts of the Low Country, rolling hills of the Piedmont region, and the forested peaks of the Blue Ridge Mountains.

Tennessee - Known for its varied terrains ranging from the Blue Ridge Mountains in the east to the fertile plains along the Mississippi River.

Texas– Includes diverse geographical features from the Gulf Coastal Plains, Interior Lowlands, Great Plains, and Basin and Range Province. These regions vary widely and contribute to the state's vast and differing landscape.

Virginia - The state's features include low-lying lands, rolling hills, mountains with elongated ridges and valleys, and water features such as numerous rivers and streams making it very topographically diverse.

West Virginia - Has two major regions: the Appalachian Plateau Province, characterized by rugged landscapes, and the Ridge and Valley Province, featuring long parallel ridges and valleys.

Observation Notes

DIXIE PIXIES

DIXIE PIXIES

Pixies, fairies, sprites, and other magical small flying creatures are common throughout the Southern United States and all originate from the realm of the faerie. This grouping of mythical creatures is referred to as the "dixie pixies". The southern dixie pixies are a large and diverse group of supernatural beings.

While there are differences in the types of dixie pixies, they do have common characteristics. First, they all have magical powers. The manifestation of the powers varies depending on the type of creature. Some have the ability to affect the forest's plant life while others can use their powers to impact human and animal interactions. Finally, they are all very small, ranging between two inches to twelve inches in height.

As a point of clarification, you may notice the difference in the spelling of the word faerie versus fairy in this section. While the words are sometimes used synonymously, the distinction is that the word faerie generally refers to the realm of the fae and any creature associated with it, while the word fairy refers to the specific creatures which are described as small winged magical beings, such as the blueberry fairy described herein.

The mostly benevolent dixie pixies have a strong connection to nature. With their magical powers they are able to affect the forest environment in many positive ways. Though they are mostly doing positive things in the forest, these creatures are also known to have a mischievous streak. Their trickery can materialize in the form of a prank or even in the altering of reality – such as the bending of time. Dixie pixies are also able to perform varying acts of cunning and even subterfuge. And while they are generally good natured, it is quite unwise for a human to cross or intentionally aggravate a dixie pixie, as the response could be rather unpleasant for the offending individual. Consider the fool who tried to keep a dixie pixie as a pet some time ago: on awakening one morning to brush his teeth, he discovered that his pearly whites had been turned a fluorescent pink! This was undoubtedly a curse set upon him by his magical captive.

SOUTHERN BELLE PIXIE

The southern belle pixie is not really a class or category of pixies, rather it is a personality type defined by a number of common characteristics. The southern belle pixie refers to a type of faerie who is concerned with proper faerie behavior, attire, and etiquette. Always polite, the southern belle pixie is known for its grace and charm.

Of course, everyone knows that pixies have magical powers and the southern belle pixie is no exception. In the magical forest, the southern belle pixie is known to wake up the beautiful meadow flowers just on passing by and it is believed that this pixie has mystical match-making skills. So when a young individual encounters one of these sprites they can engage the pixie to cast a 'magic spell' over any person of their choosing to create a strong attraction to the individual in question.

Because southern belle pixies are always prim and proper, they can be accused of being snobbish and aloof. But this is not an entirely fair description, because many of these colorful creatures are very sweet, caring, and courteous.

FACT SHEET:

<u>Category</u>: Dixie Pixie.

<u>Habitat</u>: Forests and meadows.

<u>Location</u>: Throughout the South.

<u>Diet</u>: Nuts and berries.

<u>Communication</u>: Pixies have their own unique language that they use to communicate among themselves. When communicating with humans, they are very hard to hear due to their small size, so they will use whistles and gestures to get attention.

<u>Attributes</u>: Approximately 6 inches tall with wings, antennae, with varying skin tones (blue, green, pink, brown, etc.).

PINE SPRITE

The tiny pine sprite has a positive impact on the mystical forest. Not only does it help with sowing seeds for the various trees and plants, it also helps to keep destructive creatures such as slugs, aphids and beetles at bay. This diligent work helps keep the forest strong and the magical forces within vibrant.

While the sprite is known for its beneficial impact on the forest domain, it must be stated that they do tend to have a mischievous streak. For example, if you have ever been hiking through the woods and been pelted by a falling stick or acorn, it is entirely possible that the projectile was thrown by a pine sprite. It is even possible that it was launched by a team of sprites manning a slingshot. Nevertheless, these acts are generally harmless as the projectiles tend to be very small and are able to cause very little harm.

Of course the pine sprite is not without its natural enemies: raccoons, birds of prey, and other forest predators are known to enjoy the flavor of sprites, so the sprites must be forever vigilant to avoid becoming a tasty afternoon snack.

FACT SHEET:

<u>Category</u>: Dixie Pixie.

<u>Habitat</u>: Deep forest.

<u>Location</u>: Throughout the South.

<u>Diet</u>: Insects, slugs, small lizards, nuts and berries.

<u>Communication</u>: Pine sprites have their own unique language that they use to communicate among themselves. They do not communicate with humans.

<u>Attributes</u>: Approximately 4 inches tall, with wings and a typically a blue-gray skin tone.

BLUEBERRY FAIRY

The sweet and kindly blueberry fairy is known for its ability to bring life into barren areas of the forest. Flying through the meadows, this fairy looks for wild blueberry plants. When she spots a blueberry patch, she hovers over it and chants a magical spell. It is believed that this incantation helps the plants to flourish and grow. But not only does this help the blueberry plants, the lingering magical effect of the incantation also helps the other plants around it.

It is said that the blueberry fairy has a magical connection to nature, and like all fairies she is a friend to the butterflies and the bees. This friendship helps more than just the blueberry bushes in the meadows. It also helps the other plants that need the attention of these pollinating insects.

Sighting a blueberry fairy is a very rare thing indeed, and sometimes a butterfly or a small bird are mistaken for the blueberry fairy. However, should you be fortunate enough to encounter a real blueberry fairy, you may also benefit from her magic!

FACT SHEET:

<u>Category</u>: Dixie Pixie.

<u>Habitat</u>: Forests and meadows.

<u>Location</u>: Throughout the South.

<u>Diet</u>: Nuts and berries.

<u>Communication</u>: Fairies have their own unique language that they use to communicate among themselves. When communicating with humans, they are very hard to hear do to their small size, so they will use whistles and gestures to get attention.

<u>Attributes</u>: Approximately 6 inches tall, with wings, and with varying skin tones (blue, green, pink, brown, etc.)

SWEET TEA PIXIE

The sweet tea pixie is quite common in the southern United States and is known for its hospitality, and kindness; however, it is known most especially for the delicious drink for which it is named. Collecting the nectar from the various flowering plants in the magical forest, the sweet tea pixie creates a mystical faerie brew. Forest creatures who imbibe this brew, become playful, peppy, and also a little silly.

Even in small doses, the brew itself is quite powerful. In fact, just a small drop placed in a pitcher of human tea can create a magical effect. Humans who have consumed it find that for a time they become ridiculously jovial, giggly and giddy. This pixie, so well-known for its magical concoctions, is also one of the nicest of all of faerie kind. Always positive and uplifting, the sweet tea pixie is known to say encouraging and supportive things like: "Ain't you precious!" and "Well, bless your sweet little heart!" or "Y'all come on over and join us, we have plenty of room!". It is said that even the very sight of a sweet tea pixie will put you in a great mood. While you may never encounter one yourself, if you happen to feel particularly frolicsome after drinking a glass of your Aunt Edna's sweet tea, it is possible that you may have just imbibed a "pixie spiked" refreshment!

FACT SHEET:

<u>Category</u>: Dixie Pixie.

<u>Habitat</u>: Forests and meadows.

<u>Location</u>: Throughout the South.

<u>Diet</u>: Nuts and berries.

<u>Communication</u>: Pixies have their own unique language that they use to communicate among themselves. When communicating with humans, they are very hard to hear due to their small size, so they will use whistles and gestures to get attention.

<u>Attributes</u>: Approximately 6 inches tall, with wings, antennae, with varying skin tones (blue, green, pink, brown, etc.).

Observation Notes

SWAMP CRITTERS

SWAMP IMP

In the heart of a typical southern swamp, where the air hangs heavy with humidity and the cypress trees stretch their gnarled limbs toward the murky water, there resides an elusive creature known as the swamp imp.

The swamp imp is a mischievous sprite, about the size of a small cat, with skin the color of moss and big googly eyes that help it to see on a moonless night. It thrives among the forgotten remnants of lost travelers— abandoned hats, rusted lanterns, and half-sunken rowboats.

When the sun dips below the horizon, casting long shadows across the water, the swamp imp emerges from its hiding place. Where the mist is thick and the Spanish moss drapes low, it whispers forgotten lullabies to the frogs and crickets, and it dances on lily pads, its laughter echoing throughout the cypress groves.

It is said, lucky is the traveler who spots a swamp imp, this is because the little trickster has been known to guide lost souls back to their moonlit trails, its tiny hand pointing the way to safety.

So next time you find yourself in the depths of a dark and foreboding swamp, remember that the elusive swamp imp may have its eyes on you, watching any of your missteps in anticipation that it may need to help you navigate your way out of the murky wilderness.

FACT SHEET:

<u>Category</u>: Swamp Critters.

<u>Habitat</u>: Swamps and bogs.

<u>Location</u>: Marshlands and swamps throughout the South.

<u>Diet</u>: Bugs, small fish, small reptiles and amphibians, swamp grass and swamp vegetation

<u>Communication</u>: High pitched singing, nods and hand gestures (pointing and gesturing when helping lost travelers).

<u>Attributes</u>: With its short wings, agile and dexterous limbs, and slick scaly skin, the swamp imp is the rare creature that can swim, climb and fly. Generally shy by nature, it is a nocturnal being that stays hidden during the daylight hours.

GRANDPAPPY SNAPPY

In every average pond, lake, stream or river in the south, there are turtles. Among the more prominent species is the snapping turtle. This turtle, with its large head and long tail, sports menacing hooked jaws. These jaws enable the snapping turtle to satisfy a diverse appetite which includes a wide variety of both plants and animals. Among other things, the turtle's diet includes small water creatures such as worms, crayfish, and insects, as well as rodents, and small reptiles.

In native American mythology the snapping turtle is respected for its strength and adaptability and is said to be a symbol of wisdom, and interconnectedness. It is

FACT SHEET:

Category: Swamp Critters.

Habitat: Most bodies of water—lakes, ponds, rivers, streams, swamps, etc.

Location: South Georgia, Most of Florida, South Alabama, South Mississippi, South Louisiana, and South Texas.

Diet: Bugs, small fish, small reptiles and amphibians, swamp grass and swamp vegetation.

Communication: Communicates with all turtles in a common turtle language. Can also communicate with humans in English (with a deep southern accent).

Attributes: Appears to be a very large snapping turtle, however when approached, and not threatened, Grandpappy Snappy will stand on its two hind legs and discuss whatever topic is relevant.

rumored that in any significant body of water, there is a great and wise creature who is called the grandpappy snappy. Grandpappy snappy is highly intelligent and is believed to be able to shape shift from its turtle form to a nearly humanoid appearance that walks on two legs. While grandpappy snappy can well defend itself, it is usually a blessing to encounter one, due to the enlightening interaction that may occur. In fact, many seekers have intentionally sought the advice of the creature. So if you find yourself in need of counselling, perhaps you might venture over to one of the ponds or rivers near your own home to gain the insight that grandpappy snappy can provide.

OOGLEY BOOGLEY

The oogley boogley is a mythical creature that is said to live in the forests, swamps and bayous of the deep south. Believed to be indigenous in nature, the oogly boogley stands about one foot tall with a frog-like body, slimy green skin, and webbed feet. Though it is generally harmless the

mischievous oogley boogley can appear to be a fierce adversary in spite of its diminutive stature adorned in native attire. The oogly boogley is believed to live in small communities of around thirty to forty individuals. While there is little evidence of these communities in the wilderness, it is said that small abandoned villages with tiny little huts have been located in past.

FACT SHEET:

Category: Swamp Critters.

Habitat: Swamps and bogs.

Location: South Georgia, Most of Florida, South Alabama, South Mississippi, South Louisiana, and South Texas.

Diet: Bugs, small fish, swamp grass and swamp vegetation.

Communication: The oogley boogley have their own language and can communicate with frogs and toads. They do not communicate with humans.

Attributes: The oogley boogley are clearly related to frogs and can easily disguise themselves as a bullfrog. As they are tribal in nature, they adorn themselves with brightly colored clothing, decorated with beads and feathers. For protection from predators, they carry crude weapons.

Observation Notes

VARMINTS

SQURGLAR

You just filled your new bird feeder with the best bird seed available at the market to support your local bird population with fresh and healthy food. But when you come out to look at the feeder the following day, you find that it is now empty! You look around and bird seed is scattered about on the ground. The amount in the feeder should have lasted a few weeks, and now nothing remains. What in the world has happened?

You begin to suspect that something nefarious has occurred. There are not enough birds in your neighborhood to eat that much seed. Someone or something has raided the feeder and whoever it was, is no amateur. In fact, you suspect that this was the work of the sneaky squrglar. The squrglar is practically indistinguishable from your typical southern gray squirrel with the exception of a mask and some thieving tools. But as wiley as the gray squirrel is, the squrglar is even more effective at raiding bird feeders.

While there are many techniques to keep the squrglar at bay, they are unlikely to be completely successful. This is because the squrglar is a master thief. So just realize that there is no bird feeder that the squrglar cannot pillage and there is always a risk of your bird seed being stolen right out from under your eyes.

FACT SHEET:

Category: Varmints.

Habitat: Anywhere with a good stand of trees.

Location: Found throughout the South.

Diet: Anything they can pilfer from the backyard bird feeder. They eat nuts, seeds, fruits, berries and vegetables.

Communication: The squrglar can communicate with other squirrels. Any communication with humans comes out in squeaks and squawks.

Attributes: Appears to be a large gray squirrel. May be seen toting a bag of birds seed (loot). Generally wears a mask to hide its identity.

SHARPANA

The sharpana is a mystical cat-like animal that is approximately the size of a standard house cat with varying colors and patterns of fur. If spotted in your yard, this creature can easily be confused with a neighbor's cat. However, the sharpana is far from the run of the mill tabby. This is because it is believed that the sharpana possesses magical powers. In fact, unlike the common black cat who purportedly gives you bad luck if one crosses your path, it is believed that when a sharpana crosses your path, one is blessed with a full week of serendipitous luck!

The sharpana is very difficult to spot and additionally, because it is so elusive, it is said to have the ability to make itself invisible. And while it is not known whether it can truly vanish like the famous Cheshire cat, it is practically impossible to capture a sharpana, as there is no record of one ever being taken into captivity.

But is the sharpana truly a cat? With its odd markings and ridges running down the back, some believe that it is combination of animals such as part alligator or lizard. One thing is for certain, the sharpana is a very special creature.

FACT SHEET:

<u>Category</u>: Varmints.

<u>Habitat</u>: Forest land, suburban neighborhoods.

<u>Location</u>: Sharpanas have been seen in each of the southern states.

<u>Diet</u>: Mostly small rodents and fish.

<u>Communication</u>: Communicates with other sharpana through telepathic means. Also can communicate with any type of cat including lions and tigers using telepathy. Cannot speak to humans.

<u>Attributes</u>: From a distance the Sharpana is easily mistaken for a common house cat, but on closer observation, it has odd markings and fins on its back—like a reptile. It is believed that its eyes will glow yellowish white just before becoming invisible.

MUSHROOPLE

Deep in the dark, musty forest, lives a type of creature known as the mushroople. Closely resembling a mushroom, the mushroople is a cross between plant and animal. The mushroople is truly "a fungus among us". And while it is well disguised from unwanted observation, due to the fact that it looks exactly like a mushroom, you would not want to eat a mushroople as they are incredibly poisonous. Additionally, when captured, the mushroople lets out a high-pitched wail intended to alert other mushrooples of lurking danger.

Because they are so well disguised, it is quite likely that you have mistaken a mushroople for an actual mushroom as you were hiking on a local nature trail. This is because mushrooples are prevalent throughout the South. You may have seen a ring of mushrooples in a neighbor's yard on a warm summer morning, not realizing that what you thought were mushrooms was actually a small band of mushrooples standing perfectly still trying to avoid detection.

While it would be terribly dangerous to eat a mushroople due the high content of poison, mushrooples are actually quite harmless. In fact, they are very beneficial to the environment, because they help improve the forest's soil by breaking down the fallen branches and leaves from the trees and other foliage.

FACT SHEET:

Category: Varmints.

Habitat: Forest, fields, meadows, suburban lawns.

Location: Throughout the South.

Diet: Dirt.

Communication: It is believed that the mushroople can communicate telepathically among themselves. There is no evidence that they can communicate with humans.

Attributes: Generally 3 to 5 inches tall. Mushrooples come in a variety of color variations, with a typically darker cap and lighter stem.

SOUTHERN CAVERN CRAWLER

The southern cavern crawler is an elusive, humanoid-like animal that lives in the dark and damp caves of the Appalachian Mountains and other southern mountain ranges. It has a slimy gray-green body, with a flat nose, and big ears that help it navigate in the pitch black of the caverns. Its segmented tail helps it keep its balance to deftly move through the slippery caves where it dwells and its two bulging eyes help it see in the lightless conditions. This critter feeds on insects, fungi, rodents and small fish as well as roots that grow in the underground domain.

The cavern crawler is very shy and timid, and will hide from any potential threat. It rarely ventures out of its cavernous abode and is a rare sight for humans, as it

FACT SHEET:

Category: Varmints.

Habitat: Caves and caverns.

Location: Any of the southern mountain ranges.

Diet: Bats, bugs, small fish, small reptiles and amphibians. Also mosses, lichens, and fungi that grow in the low light conditions.

Communication: It is not known if these solitary creatures have a language of their own.

Attributes: Greyish blue skinned. Large eyes to help them see in the dark cavern. Thin and agile with a tail to help their balance.

only comes out at night and avoids noisy and bright places. And while it is seldom seen, cave explorers claim that this unusual creature makes its presence known by howling and moaning when it feels that its solitary space has been violated.

VIGILARMENT

Forests throughout the south are under constant stress. Sometimes this is from over-harvesting trees, other times it's from the impact of invasive species, and often it is from commercial development. While there are programs designed to help mitigate the impact of these issues, it is said that there is a mystical creature out there who sees its purpose as being a protector of the forest. This creature is the vigilarment - an ever-vigilant friend of the forest domain.

The surly vigilarment resembles a cross between a badger and a porcupine. It is pugnacious and stubborn by nature. It has to be, since its mission is to help protect the natural environment from challenging problems. And while it is hard to describe specifically how the vigilarment operates, it is believed that much of it is done through behind-the-scenes involvement.

Some believe that the vigilarment does not even exist - that a creature born to protect the forest is just a nice fantasy; that protecting the forest is the responsibility of the citizens and not the forest dwellers. And this may be true, but if the citizens, aren't taking care of the problem, who is left to save our precious resources? But even if the vigilarment is real, we know that it is extremely rare with a tremendous task in front of it. A task too big for one species alone. So just remember, the vigilarment needs our help!

FACT SHEET:

<u>Category</u>: Varmints.

<u>Habitat</u>: Any natural and untouched area.

<u>Location</u>: Throughout the South.

<u>Diet</u>: Eats nuts and wild vegetation.

<u>Communication</u>: The language of the vigilarment is unknown, but when an area is threatened with unnecessary development, the vigilarment is known to growl and grunt ferociously.

<u>Attributes</u>: Due to the spiky quills it has on its back, the vigilarment is thought to be related to the porcupine. But with its stocky build and tenacious nature it possesses the spirit of the wolverine.

Observation Notes

SOUTHERN CREEPSTERS

HAINT

A haint is a lost ghost-like soul who has not left this world and remains to harass the living. Restless by nature and with general malicious intent, haints are known to create great stress to those who are affected by them. While it is believed that the name originated from inhabitants of the Carolina coast, the existence of haints can be traced throughout the south.

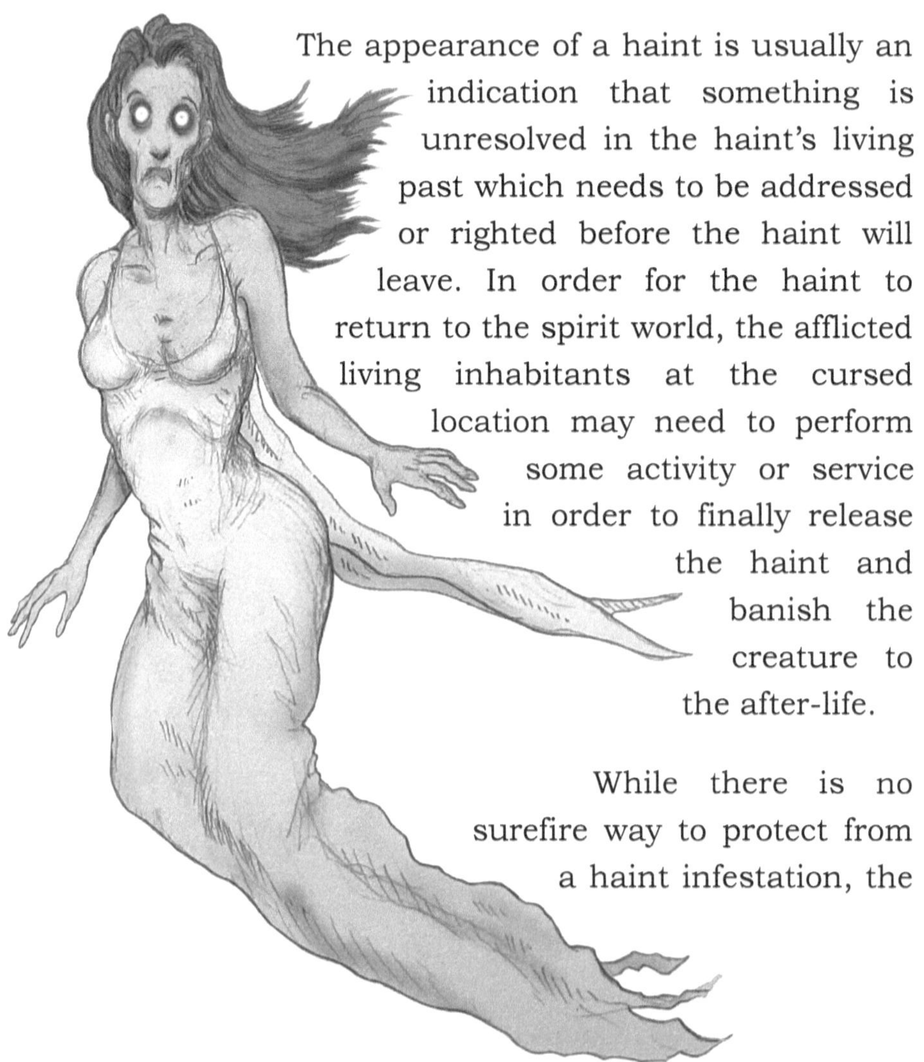

The appearance of a haint is usually an indication that something is unresolved in the haint's living past which needs to be addressed or righted before the haint will leave. In order for the haint to return to the spirit world, the afflicted living inhabitants at the cursed location may need to perform some activity or service in order to finally release the haint and banish the creature to the after-life.

While there is no surefire way to protect from a haint infestation, the use of blue paint called "haint blue" on doors, shutters, porch roofs and other parts of the home may prove effective in discouraging these ghouls from entering a structure. It is believed that the blue color of the paint resembles lake or ocean water, which is a well known deterrent, and since it is firmly established that supernatural beings cannot cross over bodies of water, it is believed that the paint will deter the haint from accessing the home and affecting the occupants.

FACT SHEET:

<u>Category</u>: Southern Creepsters.

<u>Habitat</u>: Old buildings—homes, barns, churches, graveyards, etc.

<u>Location</u>: Throughout the South. Most likely to be found in historic older cities, like Charleston, Savannah, or New Orleans.

<u>Diet</u>: Not applicable.

<u>Communication</u>: Moans, groans, icy high pitched wails. Haints rarely speak, but when they do it will be in the language they used on the earthly plain.

<u>Attributes</u>: Haints are ethereal with no real material form. Resembling the person they were when they were alive, haints are typically translucent with the ability to pass through physical structures such as walls and doors.

KUDZOO MONSTER

Many years ago a fast growing vine was imported from the country of Japan and planted in the South. This vine grew so fast that it started to cover up many acres of southern land. It grew so much that to this day, it has not stopped growing.

You have probably seen it yourself. If you are driving along a remote and lonely southern highway it can be observed along the roadside where the trees are engulfed by vines. You will also notice the ominous shape these devoured trees have taken. The sight of these behemoths may make you a bit uncomfortable and may stir a little fear within you.

It is said that sometimes late at night in the deep south, one can hear these behemoths come to life and

FACT SHEET:

<u>Category</u>: Southern Creepsters.

<u>Habitat</u>: Forests and fields.

<u>Location</u>: South Georgia, Most of Florida, South Alabama, South Mississippi, South Louisiana.

<u>Diet</u>: Trees, bushes, and anything near it.

<u>Communication</u>: Unknown.

<u>Attributes</u>: Resembles a typical kudzu patch, but has monstrous characteristics, such as glowing eyes, large powerful arms, and gnashing teeth.

move about. Their loud footsteps may be mistaken as distant thunder. So many stories of shambling masses of kudzu vines have circulated, that they are hard to ignore.

Reports from Alabama and Mississippi are common. With one particularly large one being spotted that locals refer to it as "Kudzilla".

MOUNTAIN MONSTER

The giant horned southern mountain monster is a fearsome creature that dwells in the hidden peaks of the southern smokey mountains. It has a massive body covered with fur, two powerful legs, long arms with sharp claws, and a stout tail that this beast uses to whip its prey. However, its most prominent feature is its four spindly horns that curve upwards from its head. The menacing horns are used for both defense and offense, as the monster can ram, gore, or toss anything that threatens it. This creature is territorial and aggressive and may attack any intruder that enters its domain. It is believed to feed on large animals such as bears, deer, wild boar, and sometimes even humans.

The mountain monster is rarely seen by people, and no clear photographs exist as it prefers to stay hidden in the clouds and mist. However, some brave adventurers have tried to hunt it down, either for glory or for its prized horns. While there are no known successful attempts to capture this beast, it is believed that a number of so called hunters have perished in their foolish attempts.

FACT SHEET:

Category: Southern Creepsters.

Habitat: Mountains and foothills.

Location: Any southern mountain range.

Diet: A carnivorous fiend, the mountain monster eats any wild animal it can get in its grasp. Additionally, it is believed to prey upon livestock when it is really hungry and its natural food source is diminished.

Communication: Unknown.

Attributes: Large (10 to 12 feet tall) with four horns, powerful arms and claws, and a long reptilian tail.

TROLLS

Trolls are not uncommon in the Southern United States, and it would do the reader a disservice if they were not included in this book. While there are a number of varieties in the South, the two most common are the trailer troll and the forest troll. The trailer troll is unique to its environment while the forest troll is a broader category of trolls which includes forest trolls, mountain trolls, cave trolls, and bridge trolls.

Each class of troll has its specific characteristics and inclinations, however, the commonality among them is that all trolls are nasty and disgusting creatures—the real ones at any rate! It is well known that some trolls will turn to stone if they are exposed to sunlight for too long, however, this is not always true, as is the case of the trailer troll and a number of other varieties. The following pages discuss the two most common varieties: the trailer troll and the forest troll.

FACT SHEET:

<u>Category</u>: Southern Creepsters.

<u>Habitat</u>: Caves, underneath bridges, high in the mountains, deep in the forest, abandon places like old mills, trailer parks, low-rent apartments.

<u>Location</u>: Throughout the South.

<u>Diet</u>: Trolls eat anything and everything, including humans.

<u>Communication</u>: Broken English with a southern drawl.

<u>Attributes</u>: Trolls are typically very large with big noses and pointed ears. Not known for good hygiene, a troll can often be identified in advanced, just based on their vulgar smell alone.

TRAILER TROLL

The most common type of troll in the Southern United States by far is the trailer troll. A trailer troll is a nasty and often grumpy creature that lives in a run down trailer park on the rougher side of town. Similar to its European cousin, it has a large and hairy body, with yellow teeth, sunken eyes, and a long nose. The trailer troll wears dirty and torn shirts, and jeans that barely fit. This creature spends much of its time watching bad TV shows, drinking beer, and eating junk food. It rarely leaves its trailer, except to scare away anyone who comes near it. It likes to throw rocks, bottles, rotten fruit, and insults at anyone who passes by, and generally causes trouble for its neighbors.

FACT SHEET:

<u>Category</u>: Southern Creepsters.

<u>Habitat</u>: Trailer parks.

<u>Location</u>: Throughout the South.

<u>Diet</u>: Junk food, frozen dinners and beer.

<u>Communication</u>: Loud grunting English with a southern drawl.

<u>Attributes</u>: Grayish blue to grayish green skin. Pointed ears with bad breath and yellowish teeth. Large and stocky. Can get over 7 feet tall and weigh 300 to 400 pounds.

The trailer troll hates almost everyone and is despised by the local people in the trailer park. A word of caution: do not let your child's ball roll onto its small plot of land, because the troll may try to eat it (the ball, not the child, of course!).

FOREST TROLL

The term forest troll refers to a broader category of trolls which includes forest trolls, mountain trolls, cave trolls and bridge trolls.

All of these types of trolls are essentially the same species, however, due to their chosen environment they are identified by the location in which they have chosen to live. Regardless of which type you may have the misfortune of stumbling upon, you should know that they are all equally terrifying. This is because forest trolls are large and nasty. Fortunately, they are not very smart and can be tricked fairly easily. Individuals who encounter any forest troll are possibly in dire danger, but through cunning and guile, one can easily outsmart these slow witted creatures.

Due to their aversion to sunlight, a forest troll rarely departs its home during daylight hours. One way to outsmart a troll might be to try to trick the troll into coming out of its dark lair, thereby exposing it to harmful sunlight and turning it into stone.

If that is not an option, then there are a number of

other ways that a troll can be fooled. First, since confrontations with trolls are generally rare, the troll may be just as surprised about the encounter as the individual who has stumbled on the troll. So just by confidently excusing oneself and then backing out of the situation a clean escape may be made.

If this strategy is unsuccessful, one might pretend that they are familiar with the troll and attempt to befriend the lonely soul. If the troll falls for this, then as long as the troll is not hungry, the troll may let the individual depart unscathed.

Finally, if all else fails, humor has been shown to be very effective as a deterrent to troll attacks. It is therefore recommended to memorize a few jokes to tell before wandering off into an area where a troll might be encountered.

FACT SHEET:

<u>Category</u>: Southern Creepsters.

<u>Habitat</u>: Deep forest, mountains, caves, bridges.

<u>Location</u>: Throughout the South.

<u>Diet</u>: Wild game, forest fauna, lost travelers.

<u>Communication</u>: Some forest trolls speak English, however, being generally wild, many speak only a native troll dialect.

<u>Attributes</u>: Skin tones vary from gray, to green to blue. Pointed ears with a large nose. Large and stocky. Larger than the typical trailer troll at 7 to 8 feet tall and weighing between to 400 and 500 pounds.

RIVER MONSTER

Throughout the deep south, there abound tales of great river and lake monsters. While the descriptions of these creatures vary depending on the location, the most common features indicate a resemblance to the prehistoric plesiosaur. For example, one such beast is a legendary animal that is said to lurk in the depths of the Savannah River. This creature has a long neck, a round body, flippers for swimming, and a slimy tail. In most of the locations where these monsters are said to dwell, they live in the murky depths of their watery home. It is clear that these beasts must be very stealthy, agile and

---

FACT SHEET:

Category: Creepy Critters.

Habitat: Large bodies of water.

Location: Large southern rivers and lakes.

Diet: Fish, alligators, turtles, aquatic vegetation.

Communication: Unknown.

Attributes: Appears to look similar to the ancient plesiosaur, with fins, a long neck and tail. A very fast swimmer to enable it to capture its aquatic prey.

---

can move swiftly through the water. Their swimming prowess allows them to capture any aquatic prey with ease.

Since this type of creature is extremely rare, only a few eyewitnesses have reported seeing one. One reason for the scarcity of sightings may be that these creatures generally will only surface when the river or lake is dark, calm and quiet.

ROUGARU

Deep in the murky swamps of Cajun Louisiana, roams the cursed rougarou. The name "rougarou" is a derivation of the French "loup-garou" - a French werewolf. The rougarou is very much like the common werewolf with its transformation of a human into a ferocious wolf-beast. It is rumored that a person who has broken their religious Lenten vows must live as a werewolf-like creature and bear this malady for 101 days until they can draw the blood of another person to pass along the curse. Until then, the hapless soul will create havoc by attacking livestock and humans alike.

The possibility of a tragic encounter with the terrible rougarou on a moonlit night to anyone travelling the backroads of Cajun country in Louisiana is a very real concern, so it is highly recommended that one carry a piece of silver with them to help protect from this dangerous creature.

FACT SHEET:

<u>Category</u>: Creepy Critters.

<u>Habitat</u>: Swamps and bogs.

<u>Location</u>: South Louisiana.

<u>Diet</u>: Livestock, wild game, the occasional, unsuspecting human.

<u>Communication</u>: After transforming into a wolf creature there is no communication with a rougaru.

<u>Attributes</u>: Large wolf-like human with dark brown fur and glowing red eyes.

Observation Notes

LITTLE FOLK

GNOMES

Common through-out Europe and the United States the gnome is one of the most prevalent of the little folk. In the southern states the presence of a gnome around the homestead is considered good luck, however, there is little evidence to suggest that one will actually be the recipient of any luck if a family of gnomes moves onto their property.

Nonetheless, gnomes can be very helpful and friendly neighbors. First, they are good at keeping common pests under control by domesticating rodents like chipmunks, birds, and mice so they don't cause harm or infest the home. Next, they can help reduce the weeds or invasive plants on a property by cultivating them for their own use. Finally, they are just fun to have around! With their silly antics and humor, a gnome and his family can be very entertaining. Dancing, singing and even telling jokes are not uncommon activities for these jovial types. So while having gnomes on your property may not actually bring you any good fortune, it may at the very least bring you some laughter and smiles!

FACT SHEET:

<u>Category</u>: Little Folk.

<u>Habitat</u>: Gnomes make their dwellings in different locations: tree stumps, underground burrows, tree houses, small caves, stand-alone gnome huts, etc.

<u>Location</u>: Throughout the South.

<u>Diet</u>: Fruits, vegetables, breads, some meat such as fish or fowl.

<u>Communication</u>: Most southern gnomes speak English with a thick southern accent.

<u>Attributes</u>: Generally between 1 to 2 feet tall. Gnomes appear some-what portly due to their preference for heavy fattening foods.

YUMBOE

The yumboe, which has pale white skin, and silvery hair is thought to be a ghost or a spirit. However, it is possible that the yumboe is really just a type of little folk like the gnomes or elves and has been mistaken for a spirit due to its appearance and magical abilities. The yumboe is believed to have originated in Africa, but they are also known to exist in the southern United States. The American version of this creature is said to have a striped tail. Little else is known about these creatures and the living habits of the yumboe are quite a mystery. However, it is commonly believed that they abide in remote areas of the forest where it is rumored that whenever the moon is full, the yumboes will hold a great feast. It is said there is wild music and dancing at these gatherings. The yumboes are believed to love to dance! It has even been told that the yumboes have invited humans to some of these raucous parties.

The yumboe have a mischievous nature and are thought to possess magical abilities. Foremost of these is their ability to appear or disappear suddenly. Because of this skill it can be nearly impossible to actually capture a yumboe who are known to occasionally pop into a home and borrow household items without asking permission. In spite of this, Yumboes can also be quite helpful to humans and have been known to help with chores around the homestead and have even been known to help locate lost pets or children.

FACT SHEET:

Category: Little Folk.

Habitat: It is believed that the yumboe live deep in the forest.

Location: Throughout the South.

Diet: Fruits, vegetables, and wild meats.

Communication: Yumboes have their own language, but are also able to speak English.

Attributes: Pale skin with silvery blue or pink hair. They have a tail resembling that of a zebra.

AGRIGREMLIN

The agrigremlin is a little more laid back than its cousin, the gremlin. While it is still quite a mischievous devil, it is generally non-violent and is typically not excessively disruptive. However, the agrigremlin does relish causing a little bit of mayhem. They are commonly found around farms, construction sites, and other industrial installations throughout the South. The agrigremlin relishes creating havoc by disassembling, stealing, or causing minor sabotage. Examples of its actions can be disconnecting the battery leads on a tractor or truck, pulling a circuit breaker in a warehouse, or causing some other distraction.

FACT SHEET:

<u>Category</u>: Little Folk.

<u>Habitat</u>: Farms, construction sites, and other industrial installations.

<u>Location</u>: Throughout the South.

<u>Diet</u>: Anything growing on the farm that they have inhabited.

<u>Communication</u>: Unknown.

<u>Attributes</u>: Approximately 3 feet tall. Greenish skin, small horns and a tail. Wears workman like clothing: jeans, boots, work shirt.

Why does the agrigremlin do such things? Maybe it has gotten bored and is looking for a little excitement. Maybe it wants some attention, or maybe it is simply curious. It is hard to know the reasons for these annoying acts.

The agrigremlin stands between two and three feet tall, is ultra-quick and nearly impossible to catch. Once a place has been hexed with the presence of one of these annoying beings, it is very hard to be rid of them. The best thing to do if you find that you have been afflicted with the presence of an agrigremlin is to simply ignore it. Though this seems counterintuitive, if ignored (aside from fixing the problems the agrigremlin has created), the agrigremlin will eventually leave and find other victims to aggravate.

SOUTHERN LEPRECHAUN

Similar to its Irish cousin, the southern leprechaun is a magical being who stands about three feet tall. Like the leprechauns of the old country, the southern leprechaun loves the color green and has a wardrobe of green jackets, pants and hats.

While the southern leprechaun is quite a rare breed, they are found throughout the south. The highest concentrations are known to, live in and around Savannah, Georgia whose annual St. Patiricks Day celebration is one of the biggest in the United States.

Like their Irish forebears southern leprechauns are famous for hording gold. It is rumored that following the War Between the States, that much of the treasure from

FACT SHEET:

Category: Little Folk.

Habitat: It is a magical secret where leprechauns live.

Location: Throughout the South, with high concentrations near Savannah, Georgia.

Diet: Typical Irish fare—potatoes, corned beef, shepherd's pie, green beer, whiskey.

Communication: Southern leprechauns speak English with a thick southern accent.

Attributes: Generally between 2 to 4 feet tall. Red hair wearing green clothing.

the defeated South was lost. The truth may be that large portions of this treasure were in fact absconded by these sprites. So if you are ever lucky enough to encounter a southern leprechaun and find the pot of gold at the end of the rainbow, you may discover that you are looking at the missing treasure of the Southern Confederacy.

COBLIN

Hiding in an abandoned homestead off a forgotten dirt road is where you may find a small colony of coblins. These nasty creatures are closely related to their horrible European cousins, the goblins and they are every bit as awful. Usually living in a group of 10 to 15 individuals, these communities can grow to over 200. Coblins are known to live in the forgotten areas around the South: old farms, dark forests, abandoned factories- anywhere that people have deserted.

The coblin is a smallish human-like creature, with a light green complexion and pointed ears. The name coblin is derived from the merging of the words corn and goblin. They are generally dirty and unkempt wearing distressed clothing. Coblins are known for thuggery, thievery, and deception. It is not unusual to find discarded stolen items such as tv's, farm equipment and stolen vehicles near where they live. Despite their seeming disarray, coblins are quite wily and their colonies are rarely ever discovered. However, it is believed that many unsolved disappearances throughout the south may be attributable to the unfortunate discovery of a colony of coblins by an unsuspecting individual or group.

FACT SHEET:

<u>Category</u>: Little Folk.

<u>Habitat</u>: Abandoned and forgotten places.

<u>Location</u>: Throughout the South.

<u>Diet</u>: Typical southern fare.

<u>Communication</u>: Coblins speak English with a thick southern accent.

<u>Attributes</u>: Generally around 3 feet tall. Greenish skin with a sharp pointed nose and ears

---